Double or Nothing
with the Two and Only Kelly Twins

Double or Nothing
with the Two and Only Kelly Twins

Johanna Hurwitz

illustrated by
Tuesday Mourning

CANDLEWICK PRESS

Text copyright © 2017 by Johanna Hurwitz
Illustrations copyright © 2017 by Tuesday Mourning

First paperback edition 2019

Library of Congress Catalog Card Number 2017935667
ISBN 978-0-7636-8808-0 (hardcover)
ISBN 978-1-5362-0372-1 (paperback)

18 19 20 21 22 23 BVG 10 9 8 7 6 5 4 3 2 1

Printed in Berryville, VA, U.S.A.

This book was typeset in Caecilia.
The illustrations were done in watercolor.

Candlewick Press
99 Dover Street
Somerville, Massachusetts 02144

visit us at www.candlewick.com

For Uri, gone but never gone
J. H.

For Miss Amelia
T. M.

CONTENTS

Chapter One
Who's Who?
1

Chapter Two
Looking Different
11

Chapter Three
The Sleepover
21

Chapter Four
Poetry Lessons
36

Chapter Five
Hair Today, Gone Tomorrow
49

Chapter One
Who's Who?

Whoever met Arlene and Ilene Kelly had a problem. They could not tell the two sisters apart. That's because the girls were identical twins.

They were the same height and weight. Their noses were shaped exactly the same. As infants, there had been only two days separating when Ilene cut her first tooth from when Arlene showed signs of hers. And six years later, just a week separated the loss of those same two teeth. So their smiles were exactly alike. They both had brown hair, the same length, almost always worn in pigtails. They both had brown eyes and even wore the same style eyeglasses to help them see. In all their seven years of life they had almost always dressed in matching clothes.

"It's not my fault that blue is my favorite color," said Ilene.

"I can't help it if I like blue best, too," said Arlene.

No wonder almost no one knew one sister from another.

Their parents could tell them apart, of course.

"How do you do it?" the twins' friends Joey and Monty once asked Mrs. Kelly.

"I don't know. I just do," she replied,

shrugging. "After all, Joey, your mother can tell you and your brother apart."

"But my brother is three years older than I am. He wears braces. His eyes are brown and mine are blue. There are lots of ways to tell us apart."

Mrs. Kelly nodded. "True. But I'll bet your mother could still tell you apart even in the dark."

Arlene and Ilene did just about everything together. They both liked to do jigsaw puzzles. They both liked to paint pictures on their two-sided easel, and they liked to help their mother cook. They both especially loved baking cookies.

Arlene liked to have bright pink polish on her toenails. "It makes me feel fancy," she explained.

"Nail polish on your toenails is silly," said
Ilene.

Only in the summer, when they both wore
sandals without socks, could people see the
difference.

In the end, it hardly seemed to matter if

4

Joey or Monty could tell the twins apart. They all played together, rode bikes together, skated together, and walked to school together.

At school the girls were in second grade but were not in the same classroom. The school had a rule that siblings should always be separated.

"That's a silly rule," said Ilene.

"Maybe they're worried that a teacher would get confused," Arlene said.

"We could just wear name tags. Then a teacher could read our names and know which of us is which," said Ilene.

The sisters asked their parents to tell the principal about the name tags idea. "That way we could be in the same class," said Ilene.

"I'm sure there is more to it than that,"

their father said. "It's important for siblings, especially twins, to learn to be individuals."

"At least we can still walk to school together," Arlene pointed out.

"We can still eat lunch together," said Ilene.

"In the afternoon, we get to walk home together," said Arlene.

"See. You are hardly separated at all," their father said.

"But I still wish we were in the same class," said Arlene.

"Me, too," said Ilene.

Occasionally, one of the twins would wake up in the morning before the other and lie in bed thinking about the business of being an identical twin. *Maybe I'm not Ilene,* Ilene would think. *Maybe I only think I'm Ilene and I'm really Arlene.*

Arlene admitted that sometimes she woke up wondering if she was really Arlene, so she'd look at her hands and examine each finger. If she could find the tiny scar on her pinkie from the time one of their pet ferrets had bitten her, it reassured her that she was Arlene.

Anyone looking at X-rays of the two sisters could tell them apart because Ilene still had her appendix, but, not too long ago, Arlene had appendicitis. She ended up in the hospital and had to have her appendix removed.

So the X-rays of the two sisters showed the difference. But people didn't walk around carrying X-rays. And most people wouldn't recognize an appendix if they saw one, anyhow.

Ilene and Arlene almost always liked the same things. They both loved the same TV programs. They both adored French toast for Sunday breakfast.

"I'm sure there isn't a seven-year-old in this country who doesn't love French toast for breakfast," Mrs. Kelly said as she dipped the slices of bread into the egg mixture.

"Not as much as I do!" said Ilene.

"Or as much as I do," Arlene said.

But sometimes, Ilene and Arlene had surprisingly different tastes. Arlene liked purple grapes and Ilene liked green ones better. Arlene liked Golden Delicious apples and Ilene liked Red Delicious ones.

Ilene liked pink grapefruit and Arlene liked white grapefruit. Ilene liked her hamburgers well done and Arlene preferred hers a little juicier. Ilene liked white bread but Arlene preferred whole wheat.

Both girls loved chocolate ice cream. However, Ilene liked hers with chunks of extra chocolate in it while Arlene liked hers smooth, without lumps.

Sometimes at night, as they were getting ready for bed, the two sisters stood in front of the bathroom mirror and stuck out their tongues.

9

Just like their faces, their hair, and their height, their two tongues were identical. They were both the very same shade of pink.

"How come my tongue likes different things than your tongue?" asked Ilene.

Arlene shook her head. She had no answer.

"Dad likes coffee ice cream," said Ilene, "but I think it tastes like smoke."

"And Mom's favorite flavor is strawberry," said Arlene.

It was a big mystery. Bigger than telling which twin was which. No matter. Forever and ever, Ilene would be Ilene and Arlene would be Arlene. *Thank goodness for that,* Ilene thought.

Chapter Two
Looking Different

One Monday morning in early November, the Kelly family overslept. There had been a brief power failure during the night. As a result, Mrs. Kelly's alarm clock didn't go off. It was just habit that eventually woke Mrs. Kelly, half an hour late.

"No time for cereal this morning," Mrs. Kelly shouted upstairs to her daughters apologetically. The girls were getting dressed as quickly as firefighters. It was too bad they didn't have a pole to slide down into the kitchen.

They each ate a granola bar while Mrs. Kelly combed their hair into pigtails.

The girls were old enough to comb their own hair, but they still had trouble putting on the elastic bands that held their pigtails in place. Having their mother do it that day was quicker.

"Hold still, honey," said Mrs. Kelly. Ilene was trying to tie her shoelaces as her mother was combing her hair.

"Don't forget your lunches," said Mrs. Kelly as the girls grabbed their backpacks. Luckily the lunches had been packed the night before.

"What's for lunch?" asked Ilene.

"Tuna fish," said their mother. "And an apple and a box of raisins."

"I wish they were peanut-butter sandwiches," called Ilene over her shoulder as she rushed out of the house.

At the corner of their street they met up with their friends Joey and Monty to walk to school.

"Do you like peanut-butter-and-jelly sandwiches?" Ilene asked the boys.

"I love them," Monty said.

"Me, too," said Joey, smacking his lips.

Then Joey stopped and paused, looking at

the twins. Then he said, "You look different today."

"Different from what?" asked Arlene.

"Different from each other," Joey said.

"How?" Ilene asked.

Joey shrugged. "I don't know. You just do."

"I think we look just like we always do," said Arlene. "Ilene looks just like me and I look just like her."

"Joey's right," said Monty. "I can't explain it either, but you do look a little bit different today."

By this time they had reached the next corner, where the safety guard waved them to cross the street.

"I don't feel different," said Ilene.

"We slept late," said Arlene. "I didn't have time to wash my face. Maybe that's why I look different."

"But I didn't wash my face either," said Ilene. "So that doesn't explain it."

"You're wearing matching clothes and matching shoes. Your backpacks are the same color. Your hair is combed exactly the same. But something is different," insisted Joey.

"You're just saying that to confuse us," Ilene said.

"Wait a minute. Your shoelace is untied," Joey said to Ilene.

"See," said Monty, smiling. "That's one way you're different."

The girls looked down at their feet. Ilene's shoelace had come undone.

Ilene bent down and retied her shoe.

"Those are neat socks," said Monty, admiring the striped socks that peeked out from the bottom of Ilene's pants. They were

red, green, yellow, and blue. "My socks are pretty boring."

"I love these. They make me feel like dancing," Ilene said.

"Do you have them, too?" Joey asked Arlene.

Arlene showed them her socks. They were solid blue. "Socks are socks," she said. "Most of the time, no one even sees them."

"Maybe that's why we look different," said Ilene. She stood up so that her pants hid her fancy socks. "Do we look the same now?" she asked.

The boys shook their heads. "You should but you don't," said Joey.

By now they had reached the school and they saw Mr. Harris, the school librarian. He was carrying a big armload of books.

"Hi, Mr. Harris," Arlene called out.

"Well, look at that. It's my favorite identical twins," Mr. Harris greeted them.

"Did you read all those books last night?" Ilene asked in amazement.

"I bet you have to read every book in the whole library," said Arlene.

"Yep. I read these over the weekend," he admitted.

He looked at Ilene and said, "And did you lose your tooth last night or over the weekend?"

"Which tooth?" asked Ilene, but even as she spoke her tongue was searching the inside of her mouth. "Oh, no!" she said.

"What's wrong?" asked Arlene.

"I lost another tooth and I didn't even notice." A horrified expression crossed Ilene's face. "I must have swallowed it." Was it going

to start jumping around in her stomach? Would it chew food from inside?

"Yuck," said Arlene. "Do you think it happened when you were sleeping? Or maybe it fell out when you were chewing that granola bar."

"Here today and gone tomorrow, as they say," said Mr. Harris. "But you'll have a new tooth growing into that space in no time." He shifted the pile of books he was holding. "Well, I'll see you later," he said, and turned to go into the school.

"Are you worried that the tooth fairy won't come to your house tonight?" teased Joey.

"Puh-leeze!" said Ilene and Arlene in unison.

"Well, at least we solved the mystery," said Monty. "Now we know why you two don't look exactly the same this morning."

Arlene checked that all her teeth were still in place. Sure enough, she could feel a tooth moving a little bit. It was getting ready to fall out, too. It wouldn't be long before she and Ilene had identical smiles once again.

Chapter Three
The Sleepover

"My sister and I have an idea," Claudia Best said to Arlene one Thursday morning as they were hanging up their jackets in the back of their classroom. "We think we should all do a sleepover on Saturday night."

Claudia was a triplet. Claudia's sister, Roberta, was in Ilene's class. Their brother, Simon, was in still another second-grade class.

The two Best girls were identical, but they never dressed the same and they wore their hair in different styles. They almost didn't seem like real twins to Arlene and Ilene. All four girls were good friends.

"Great!" Arlene said. She knew her parents would say yes. "Will you come and sleep over at our house?"

"Sure!" said Claudia. "I think it will be fun to sleep in your room with the ferrets." The ferrets, Frannie and Frankie, were Arlene and Ilene's pets.

"I know we'll have so much fun, but what will Simon do?" asked Arlene.

"Simon joined the Cub Scouts and they're going on a camping trip this weekend," said Claudia.

Arlene wished it was lunchtime because she couldn't wait to tell Ilene about the Saturday sleepover.

But Roberta had already told Ilene about the Saturday sleepover idea. Ilene loved the plan.

So when it was lunchtime, the four girls sat together and got busy making plans. "There are so many games we could play," said Ilene.

"And we can borrow movies from the library," said Roberta.

"Let's get a scary one," said Claudia.

"I like funny movies better than scary ones," said Ilene.

"Me, too. Funny is better," said Arlene.

"How about pancakes for breakfast on Sunday morning?" said Roberta.

"We love pancakes," said Ilene. "Those are our absolute favorite."

"Unless we have French toast," said Arlene. "That's our other absolute favorite."

As the twins hoped, Mr. and Mrs. Kelly agreed that the four girls could have a sleepover at their house on Saturday. "You should let your guests sleep in your beds," Mrs. Kelly said. "You girls can use your sleeping bags on the floor."

Arlene and Ilene grinned at each other. Lying on the floor in a sleeping bag was fun.

"It will almost be like we're on a Cub Scout sleepover," said Arlene.

"I'm glad we're going to sleep in a house and not in the woods," said Ilene.

"Me, too," said Arlene.

Saturday morning, Ilene and Arlene straightened up their bedroom and cleaned out the ferrets' cage. The sleepover would begin at five p.m. "That way we can all have dinner together," said Ilene. "Plus we'll have lots of time to play before we go to sleep."

Mrs. Kelly made her daughters' favorite meal. The girls helped her make cupcakes for dessert, but they left them unfrosted so that the four girls could decorate them themselves.

At ten after five, the doorbell rang. It was Claudia, Roberta, and Mrs. Best. Claudia had a canvas tote bag in her hand.

The girls all danced together with excitement.

"It's nice to see how well our girls all get along," Mrs. Kelly said to Mrs. Best.

"Yes," agreed Mrs. Best. "Of course they have each other, but one can never have too many friends."

Roberta suddenly stopped dancing around and looked at the sisters. "Which of you is Ilene?" she asked, grinning.

"I am," said Ilene with a giggle. The other girls laughed, too.

The four girls ran upstairs.

When they got to Ilene and Arlene's room, Roberta said to Ilene, "Isn't it funny that you're going to be sleeping over at my house tonight and half the time I still can't even tell you apart from your sister?" she said.

"What do you mean? I'm not sleeping at your house tonight," said Ilene. "You're sleeping at my house."

"No. Don't you remember? We planned it out," said Roberta. "You're coming to my house. And Claudia is staying here at your house with Arlene."

Arlene had been petting one of the ferrets. She put him down and turned to Claudia. "Wait a minute, aren't you and Roberta both sleeping over?"

"That's not what we said," said Claudia. "We just said we'd have a sleepover."

Roberta nodded. "We meant all four of us on the same night, but split two and two."

"But Ilene and I always do everything together," said Arlene.

"Well, sometimes my sister and I like to do things separately," said Roberta. "Don't you ever feel that way?"

Ilene and Arlene shrugged. Mostly they liked doing everything together.

"Why?" asked Roberta and Claudia together.

"That's just the way we do things," said Arlene.

"I never said I'd go to your house," said Ilene. "Not tonight."

"Please come," Roberta begged Ilene.

"You'd only be away from home for a short time. Just one night and breakfast tomorrow. I know we'll have fun. I promise."

"I'll miss you," Arlene said to her sister. "But it might be fun to do something separately for a change."

Ilene took her ferret out of the cage and held it close. "Would you miss me, Fannie?" she whispered into the ferret's little ear. Ilene had never ever been separated from Arlene except when Arlene had

her appendix out and stayed for two nights in the hospital. She had missed Arlene very much. Still, she had been glad that she didn't have to stay at the hospital to keep her sister company. It would be much better to be parted from Arlene during a sleepover than to stay at a hospital.

"What's the problem, girls?" asked Mrs. Kelly, coming upstairs. She was followed by Mrs. Best.

"Ilene doesn't want to come to our house," Roberta told her mother sadly.

"It's just that I thought we were all going to stay here!" said Ilene.

"Calm down," said Mrs. Kelly. "I'm sure you'd have a really good time if you went." Then she turned to Mrs. Best. "I'm afraid there was a misunderstanding. My girls thought the four of them would all be here tonight. And that's always a possibility. But why don't you come back down to the kitchen with me," Mrs. Kelly suggested to Roberta and Claudia's mom. "Maybe the

31

girls can work this out together."

When the mothers were gone, Ilene turned to Roberta. "I have extra pajamas I could lend you if you stay here," she offered.

Then Ilene remembered that Claudia and Roberta had a huge dollhouse that their father had made for them. If there were just two girls in the room instead of four she'd get more turns playing with it. Maybe she could bring one of her dolls from home to visit the dollhouse just like she would be visiting Roberta's house. The doll would have a sleepover, too. Ilene giggled to herself.

"If you have a rotten time, you'll never have to sleep over again," Roberta promised. "But I know it will be fun. I know you'll have a really good time."

"Will you sleep over here sometime?" Ilene asked Roberta.

"Yes," said Roberta.

So in the end, Ilene packed an overnight bag with her pajamas, her toothbrush and hairbrush, and one of her favorite dolls. Mrs. Best drove her and Roberta to the Best house. Dinner at the Kelly house was spaghetti and meatballs. And—surprise, surprise—dinner at the Best house was spaghetti and meatballs, too. All four girls had the same favorite dinner.

Arlene and Claudia decorated cupcakes for dessert. Ilene and Roberta made ice-cream sundaes.

Arlene and Claudia watched a funny movie, played with the ferrets, worked on a jigsaw puzzle, and played music and danced. Ilene and Roberta played with the dollhouse, painted with watercolors, watched a cartoon, and had a pillow fight. Ilene taught Roberta

a game that she and Arlene had made up: the two girls had a staring contest, and whoever laughed first lost. Arlene taught Claudia that very same game.

All four girls washed their hands and faces. All four girls brushed their teeth and put on their pajamas. Ilene got into Claudia's bed at the Best house and Claudia got into Ilene's bed at the Kelly house. All four girls stayed awake talking and giggling for at least another hour—maybe it was two.

None of the parents knew for sure. They'd already fallen asleep.

Chapter Four
Poetry Lessons

Now that they were in second grade, Arlene and Ilene were learning about poetry. It was part of their language arts studies.

Arlene's teacher, Mrs. Storch, explained that nursery rhymes were poetry. Then she asked her students to think of rhymes that they might remember from when they were little. At first, no one raised a hand.

"Let me give you a hint," said Mrs. Storch. "How about Jack and Jill went up the . . ."

"Hill!" most of the students shouted out.

"That's right," said Mrs. Storch. "Now can you think of any others?"

"'Three Blind Mice.'"

"'Hickory Dickory Dock.'"

"'Humpty Dumpty.'"

Suddenly everyone in the class could remember a nursery rhyme. It was an exciting surprise to discover that they already knew poetry.

Meanwhile, in Ilene's second-grade class, Ms. Frost explained that poetry could be very short or very long. The teacher read a few poems aloud.

The biggest surprise was that one poem was written by a man named Robert Frost.

"Is he your brother?" one of the boys called out.

Ms. Frost laughed. "No. It's just a

coincidence that Robert Frost and I have the same last name."

"Is he your husband?" asked another student.

"No, no. He's no relation at all," said Ms. Frost.

Still, no matter what Ms. Frost said, most of the students were certain that the poet Robert Frost was her relative. Why else would she have picked one of his poems to read?

Ilene and her classmates copied some poems into their notebooks. Others they memorized.

"Listen to what I learned in school today," Ilene told her family at supper.

"A bird came down the walk:
He did not know I saw;
He bit an angle-worm in halves
And ate the fellow, raw."

"Yuck," said Arlene. She had just cut a piece of chicken cutlet and put it on her fork. "I wouldn't want to eat a raw worm."

"I wouldn't want to eat a cooked worm, either," said Ilene, "but I like that poem. It's funny. And it's easy to remember because it rhymes."

"Do you know who wrote it?" asked Mr. Kelly.

"A lady named Emily something," said Ilene. "I remember her name was Emily because there's an Emily in my class."

"There's a famous poet named Emily Dickinson," said Mrs. Kelly.

"That's who it was." Ilene remembered now. "The poet was named Emily Dickinson."

The next day, Ms. Frost taught Ilene's class

about very, very short poems called haiku. Each poem had exactly three lines. No more. No less. Ms. Frost read several haiku to her students. The first line and the third line had exactly five syllables each. The middle line always had exactly seven syllables. The three lines didn't have to rhyme. Even so, Ilene knew it wouldn't be that easy to write one. Her homework was to write a haiku.

"All haiku are about nature," Ms. Frost pointed out. "For example, it could be about a season or the weather."

"How about trees?" asked one student.

"Or flowers?" asked one of the girls.

"Or dogs?"

"Yes. Yes. Yes," said Ms. Frost. "Those are all good ideas."

"We could write a haiku about snow," said Roberta.

"Or frost," said Ilene.

Everyone laughed. Imagine writing a poem about their teacher!

Arlene came home with a different poetry assignment. She didn't have to write a poem, but she had to find one from a book. "Pick out and copy down a poem about something you can touch," Mrs. Storch had told her students.

"I don't think it's very fair," said Ilene when she heard what Arlene's homework was. "It's so much easier to pick out a poem somebody else wrote than to write one yourself."

Arlene grinned. "I guess it's my lucky day," she said. Then she added, "I'll help you write your haiku if you want."

"Oh, thanks," Ilene said. She was glad to have a sister to help her. "I guess it's my lucky day, too."

With Arlene's help, Ilene had a haiku written by the end of the week.

When it snows and snows
I feel it on my toes and
Also on my nose.

It was Arlene who suggested that the word "and" could be part of the second line to make the three lines have the right number of syllables.

Then, just for fun, the two girls wrote another poem together.

I have a sister —
She is my twin.
She's not very fat,
And she's not very thin.
When I look at her,

What do I see?

She's just like a mirror.

I see me.

Arlene's easy homework turned out not to be so easy after all. Mrs. Kelly took her daughters to the public library, where Arlene could look through lots of poetry books. Four of Arlene's classmates were at the library working on the assignment, too. They were all looking for the perfect poem about something that could be touched: daffodils, pussy willows, dandelions. Arlene wanted something more exciting than flowers.

She looked through three books before she found the perfect poem. She was sure that no one else would ever select it. The poem was by a man named William Blake and was called "The Tyger." Even though the

poet spelled the name of the animal in an odd way, Arlene knew he was writing about a tiger.

"I have it," she told Ilene, and showed her the page.

"A tyger?" said Ilene after reading the poem. "You can't touch a tiger. It's too dangerous. It would be impossible. Besides, there aren't any around here so how could you possibly touch one?"

Arlene was disappointed. She loved the tiger poem and didn't want to copy down a poem about daffodils.

Ilene saw how sad her sister looked. "Daffodils are very pretty," she said.

Arlene sat staring at the words on the page in the poetry book. Ilene sat next to her and tried hard to think of a way to help her sister. How could one possibly touch a tiger?

And then, Arlene suddenly got an idea. Almost at the same time, Ilene got an idea, too. They whispered and giggled together as Arlene began copying the tiger poem.

When she handed in her homework on Friday, Mrs. Storch shook her head. "This is a wonderful poem," she told Arlene. "And it's very famous. But you forgot about my instructions. You can't touch a tiger."

Arlene grinned. She was able to tell her teacher that there were not one or two or even three ways to touch a tiger. She listed four ways that a person could touch a tiger: "When he's a baby, when he's sleeping, when he's dead, and with a stick."

For a moment, Mrs. Storch was speechless. Then she started laughing. "I've been teaching for many years, and no one has ever come up with that argument," she said.

"You're very clever to figure that out."

Arlene smiled happily at Mrs. Storch. She bet even William Blake wouldn't have thought of four ways to touch a tiger.

baby

sleeping

dead

stick

Chapter Five
Hair Today, Gone Tomorrow

Among the girls in Arlene's class and those in Ilene's class, some had very long hair. Hannah Ross wore her blond hair in a long ponytail, Sophie Sheehan usually wore her brown hair loose, and Ellen Miller had pigtails like Arlene and Ilene, but hers were much longer. The sisters admired the hairstyles of their classmates, but they were satisfied with their small pigtails. Having shorter hair meant that it didn't take too long to dry after they washed it. And having shorter hair meant it didn't get tangled and need lots of brushing. Of course, the sisters knew that they didn't always have to wear their hair in the same way. Each could change her look if she wanted. Arlene sometimes wondered what she would look like with long, long hair. She imagined moving her head and having her hair swing back and forth. That would be so neat. Still, she just wasn't ready to let her hair start growing out yet. Then one day their hair situation changed.

It began when Mrs. Kelly noticed Ilene scratching her head as she was doing her homework.

"Stop poking at your head," she told her daughter. "You just had a shampoo last night."

"I can't help it," said Ilene. "My head is itchy."

"I feel itchy, too," agreed Arlene. She scratched the top of her head.

"Oh, no," said Mrs. Kelly. "I hope that doesn't mean what I think it means." She parted Ilene's hair with her fingers and looked.

"Oh, no," she said again.

"What is it?" asked Ilene.

"I think you have head lice," she told her daughter.

"Lice! Yuck!" said Ilene with a shudder.

"What about me? Do I have lice, too?" asked Arlene with concern.

"Probably," said her mom. She looked at Arlene's scalp, and then she sighed. "The answer is yes."

"Well, we're twins," Ilene reminded Mrs. Kelly. "We always do the same thing." It was absolutely the most awful thing in the world to have lice, Ilene thought. But it was a big, big relief to her that Arlene had them, too. At least her sister couldn't tease her about them. Not when she had them herself.

"This is a good example of a time when it would be good not to do everything alike," said Mrs. Kelly with a sigh. "But we're going to take care of this situation as fast as we can.

Get your jackets. We're going to the drugstore right now. There is a special shampoo that we can buy to get rid of the lice."

Mrs. Kelly turned off the stove where she had been preparing dinner.

So even before dinner, Arlene and Ilene washed their hair for the second night in a row. They wore clean pajamas, and Mrs. Kelly changed the sheets and pillowcases on their beds. Their blankets went into the washing machine. "Such tiny bugs, but they sure cause a lot of work," Mrs. Kelly complained.

"Where did we get them?" asked Arlene. "Did I catch them from Ilene?"

"Maybe I caught them from Arlene," said Ilene.

"Who knows?" said their mom. "There may well be many cases of them at your school."

The next day at school, the sisters each secretly presented their teachers with a note from their mother.

Ilene's teacher, Ms. Frost, read the note and made an announcement at once. "There's a possibility that some of you, most likely girls because you have longer hair than the boys, have been exposed to head lice."

Ilene was pleased that her teacher hadn't singled her out.

The boys all grinned at one another. "Thank goodness I'm not a girl," one of them called out.

"No. You're wrong there," said Mrs. Frost. "Lice don't care if they live on the scalp of a girl or a boy. So there is equal chance that everyone here has some uninvited guests on their heads."

"Gross!" said someone. Everyone felt the same.

In her classroom, Arlene blushed when Mrs. Storch made the annoucement. Luckily no one knew that she had those little creatures in her hair. Maybe they were gone by now, she hoped. She looked over at Claudia. If Claudia and Roberta and their brother, Simon, all had lice, their mom would really have a huge load of laundry to do.

Before the morning was over, Mrs. Robbins, the school nurse, examined every second-grader's head. Not just girls but boys too. Then she made an announcement in each classroom.

"Most of you have head lice. I'm going to give every student a note to take home. There is a brand of shampoo that your parents can buy at the drugstore without a prescription. If you follow the directions on the shampoo bottle, you should be able to get rid of the lice within a few days. If you don't all follow the instructions and wash with this special shampoo, you may re-infect your classmates. So it's very important to take care of this situation at once."

Cindy Webb started crying. "I don't want to have bugs on my head," she sobbed.

"No one wants to have bugs," Ms. Frost said. She gave Cindy a tissue. "Please don't cry," she begged. "Or else I might start crying, too."

"Do you have bugs?" Monty asked Ms. Frost.

Ms. Frost sat down and Mrs. Robbins examined her scalp. Mrs. Robbins nodded.

"When a teacher sits down and goes over

a workbook or a reading lesson with a student, their heads are close together," Mrs. Robbins explained. "These lice are good jumpers, so they can jump from head to head."

"I can't wait for school to be over so I can go buy that shampoo," Ms. Frost said.

Kids always say they can't wait for school to be over, but it was the first time Ilene had ever heard a teacher say that.

"And I'm going to get myself a short haircut, too," she announced.

That gave Ilene an idea.

"Can we get a haircut?" Ilene asked her mother when they went home.

"It wouldn't be a bad idea," Mrs. Kelly said after reading the school nurse's note.

"Do I have to get my hair cut?" asked Arlene as they went to the local hair salon.

"No. It's up to you," her mother said.

There were eight girls and two boys ahead of them. So instead of waiting, Mrs. Kelly took the girls to the barber shop where Mr. Kelly got his hair cut. There was only one man there ahead of them. He was getting the few hairs along the bottom of his head trimmed.

"You don't know how lucky you are," Mrs. Kelly said to the balding man as he got out of the barber's chair.

"We have head lice," Arlene announced.

The bald man rubbed his hairless scalp

and smiled. "I guess that just shows there's a good side to everything," he said.

Mrs. Kelly thought the barber might not want to touch Ilene's head. But that wasn't the case.

"Who's first?" he asked the girls. "I give a lot of crew cuts when the head lice strike."

"I don't want a crew cut," said Ilene as she climbed up into the barber's chair.

"Just joking," the barber assured the girls. He removed the rubber bands from Ilene's little pigtails and combed out her hair. "Trust me," said the barber. "No one has ever left my shop without smiling." He showed Ilene a picture of a girl with very short hair. "You'd look good with this style."

Ilene studied the picture. She liked it, so she nodded in agreement.

Arlene just watched as the barber snipped away at her sister's hair. Soon Ilene had a short pixie hairdo. She looked very cute.

Arlene looked at her sister's head. She had never considered having a pixie hairdo, but it suddenly seemed like the most wonderful style she had ever seen.

"I want my hair cut exactly like that," Arlene said to the barber.

"Are you sure?" asked Mrs. Kelly. "This is a great chance to change your look. You don't have to look like Ilene."

"I'm sure," said Arlene, pointing to Ilene. "That's the way I want my hair cut, too."

There would be plenty of time in the years ahead for her to look different from Ilene.

The next day, Arlene arrived at school to discover that half the girls in her class had new haircuts, too. Ellen Miller hadn't cut her hair, but she was wearing it in a pair of tight braids. And there was even someone else, besides Arlene, with a pixie haircut. It was her teacher, Mrs. Storch.

There were a lot of new looks in Ilene's class, too.

A new idea was beginning to develop inside each pixie-haired twin's head. Arlene and Ilene didn't always have to be mirror images of each other. Maybe next time they went shopping, they would pick clothes that didn't match. Maybe they would try different colors as well as different styles. No matter what they wore, however, or how their hair was cut, Arlene and Ilene would always be sisters. They would always be twins.

JOHANNA HURWITZ loves books, and no wonder! Her parents met in a bookstore. When she was young, they read *Stuart Little* aloud to her, and E. B. White is still one of her favorite writers. She embarked on her own writing career when she was just eight years old but would be thirty-eight before her first book was published. She is now the author of more than seventy books, including the Mostly Monty books, the beloved Riverside Kids series, and the first book about Ilene and Arlene, *The Two and Only Kelly Twins*.

Before she became a published author, Johanna Hurwitz received a master's degree in library science and worked as a children's librarian at the New York Public Library and several other libraries. She has two grown children and three grandchildren, and divides her time between Great Neck, New York, and Wilmington, Vermont. She enjoys traveling, and her goal is to travel to all fifty states. So far she has been to forty-four.

TUESDAY MOURNING grew up in Fort Collins, Colorado, where she and her eight siblings drew constantly. She looked forward to rainy days because that meant lots of time indoors for making paper dolls and creating elaborate stories about them with her sisters.

She has a bachelor of fine arts degree from Brigham Young University, where she learned how to draw and paint for a living. She has illustrated the covers of more than twenty chapter books and is the illustrator of four picture books, including the acclaimed Princess Peepers books by Pam Calvert and the popular rhyming story *Billy and Milly, Short and Silly* by Eve Feldman. When not illustrating, Tuesday Mourning loves to spend time with her husband and children, crafting, building, reading, exploring, giggling, and eating. They live in Utah.

Don't miss the first book
about the funny, lovable Kelly twins,
Ilene and Arlene,
who are truly two of a kind!

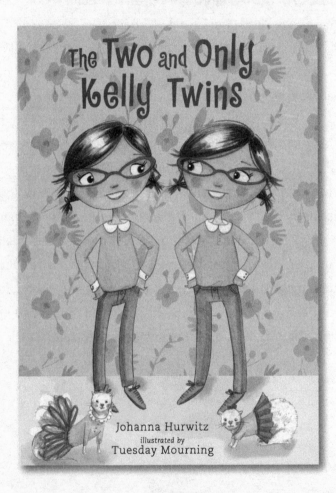

Arlene and Ilene's friend Monty has his own adventures!

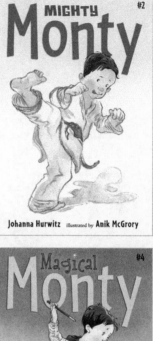

Johanna Hurwitz

illustrated by
Anik McGrory

Turn the page for an excerpt from *Mostly Monty* . . .

1

Meet Monty

This is what Montgomery Gerald Morris had:

A nickname: Monty.

A birthday on August 15. This year he had turned six.

Asthma, which sometimes made it difficult for him to breathe.

An inhaler. It was made of plastic and contained medicine. He carried it in his pocket wherever he went. If he felt that an asthma attack was coming on, he pulled it out real fast and put it in his mouth.

An excerpt from *Mostly Monty*

This is what Monty didn't have:

A brother or a sister.

A pet.

Monty also didn't have a best friend.

He didn't have any real friends at all.

It was no wonder. Because of his asthma,

he wasn't permitted to go running around outdoors like other kids. He couldn't join the Little League team. He couldn't plan to go to sleepaway camp when he got older. Who would want to be friends with a boy like him?

An excerpt from *Mostly Monty*

Monty's parents were very protective of their son. They worried about his health. Twice in the past, he'd wakened in the night unable to breathe. Both times, he had been rushed to the hospital. It sounds exciting to ride off in an ambulance with a siren and blinking lights. For Monty, it hadn't been exciting at all. It was scary. Monty didn't complain about his limitations, but he didn't like them either. Why did he have to have asthma anyhow?

An excerpt from *Mostly Monty*